JALEN'S BIG CITY LIFE

FRIENDSHIP FLOWERS

by **Dorothy H. Price** illustrated by **Shiane Salabie**

PICTURE WINDOW BOOKS
a capstone imprint

Published by Picture Window Books, an imprint of Capstone.
1710 Roe Crest Drive, North Mankato, Minnesota 56003
capstonepub.com

Library of Congress Cataloging-in-Publication Data
Names: Price, Dorothy H., author. | Salabie, Shiane, illustrator.
Title: Friendship flowers / by Dorothy H. Price : illustrated by Shiane Salabie.
Description: North Mankato, Minnesota : Picture Window Books, an imprint of Capstone, [2023] | Series: Jalen's big city life | Audience: Ages 5-7. | Audience: Grades K-1. | Summary: J.C. is going to the Spring Flower Festival with his grandparents and little sister, and he is worried that he will not get home in time to join his best friends, Amir and Vicky, at the zoo.
Identifiers: LCCN 2021047044 (print) | LCCN 2021047045 (ebook) | ISBN 9781666334975 (hardcover) | ISBN 9781666335019 (paperback) | ISBN 9781666341904 (pdf) | ISBN 9781666341959 (kindle edition)
Subjects: LCSH: African American boys—Juvenile fiction. | Grandparent and child—Juvenile fiction. | Flower shows—Juvenile fiction. | Best friends—Juvenile fiction. | CYAC: Grandparent and child—Fiction. | Flower shows—Fiction. | Best friends—Fiction. | Friendship—Fiction. | African Americans—Fiction. | LCGFT: Picture books.
Classification: LCC PZ7.1.P752828 Fr 2023 (print) | LCC PZ7.1.P752828 (ebook) | DDC [E]—dc23
LC record available at https://lccn.loc.gov/2021047044
LC ebook record available at https://lccn.loc.gov/2021047045

Editorial Credits
Editor: Alison Deering; Designer: Tracy Davies;
Production Specialist: Katy LaVigne

Design Elements
Shutterstock: Alexzel, Betelejze, cuppuccino, wormig

Printed in the United States   5553

This Book Belongs To:

munASAr mohamed

a gift from:

page ahead
children's literacy program.

www.pageahead.org

MEET J.C.

Hi! My name is Jalen Corey Pierce, but everyone calls me J.C. I am seven years old. I live with Mom, Dad, and my baby sister, Maya. Nana and Pop-Pop live in our apartment building too. So do my two best friends, Amir and Vicky.

My family and I used to live in a small town. Now I live in a city with big buildings and lots of people. Come along with me on all my new adventures!

Chapter 1

FLOWER FESTIVAL

Saturday was finally here!

J.C. was headed to the Spring Flower Festival with Nana, Pop-Pop, and Maya.

Nana used to be a botanist. She knew *a lot* about flowers.

J.C. was eager for Nana to teach him about the flowers at the festival.

But that was before Amir and Vicky called. They invited J.C. to the zoo.

"Nana, will we be back
from the flower festival by two
o'clock?" J.C. asked. "I want to
go to the zoo with my friends."

"I'm sure we will, J.C.,"
Nana replied.

Pop-Pop tucked Maya into her baby carrier. Nana packed the diaper bag. J.C. searched high and low for Ellie the Elephant. That was Maya's favorite toy.

Soon, the four of them were on their way. But when they entered the subway, J.C. knew something was wrong.

"Why are there so many people?" he asked.

"The train must be delayed," Pop-Pop said.

J.C. was worried. If they were late, they wouldn't be back in time for the zoo!

Chapter 2
DELAYED!

A few minutes later, the train arrived. Everyone crowded on.

"Pop-Pop, what time is it now?" J.C. asked.

Pop-Pop peeked at his watch. "Almost ten o'clock," he said.

"Do you think we'll still be back in time for the zoo?" J.C. asked.

"I'm sure we will," Pop-Pop replied.

Finally, J.C. and his family arrived at the Spring Flower Festival. The smell of beautiful blooms drifted through the air. Something else drifted too.

"*Ewwww!*" J.C. said. "Maya,
is that you?"

Maya giggled.

"I think somebody needs a
diaper change," said Nana.
She wrinkled her nose.

"We're not seeing any flowers until this little lady is cleaned up," Pop-Pop agreed. "I'll go do it."

J.C. frowned. Another delay! They'd definitely be late getting back for the zoo now.

Chapter 3
CITY ZOO

J.C. and Nana waited for Maya and Pop-Pop. Then J.C. noticed a large sign shaped like an arrow.

"Nana, that sign says the City Zoo is that way," J.C. said.

Nana nodded. "It sure does, J.C.! I didn't realize the Spring Flower Festival moved closer to the zoo this year."

"That means we don't have to go home," J.C. said. "Amir and Vicky can meet us here. Then we can go to the zoo!"

"That's a great idea!" Nana replied. She called Amir's and Vicky's parents to tell them.

J.C. was relieved. Now he could really enjoy the Spring Flower Festival!

Pop-Pop came back with
Maya. It was time to start
exploring.

Nana led the way through
the colorful maze. She pointed
out the different flowers.

"This is a great white

trillium," Nana explained.

"It has three petals," J.C. said.

"Trilliums are long-lasting

flowers," Nana said. "They can

live up to twenty-five years."

"Twenty-five years? That's way

older than me!" J.C. exclaimed.

Chapter 4

FRIENDSHIP FLOWERS

J.C. and his family continued through the colorful maze. They were having so much fun that J.C. forgot to worry about the time.

"J.C., Amir and Vicky will be meeting you here soon to go to the zoo," Pop-Pop reminded him.

"Can I buy something before I meet up with them?" J.C. asked.

"Of course you can," Nana answered.

J.C. found what he was looking for in the gift shop. Then he went to meet his friends. He handed Amir and Vicky their gifts.

"These are for you," J.C.
said. "They're called great white
trilliums. They have three petals,
like the three of us."

"Thanks for the beautiful
flower," Vicky said.

"It smells good too," Amir replied.

J.C. smiled. He was happy that he'd found friendship flowers at the Spring Flower Festival.

"Now we're ready for the zoo!" he exclaimed.

GLOSSARY

botanist (BOT-uh-nist)—someone who studies plants

delay (dih-LEY)—to stop or prevent for a time

eager (EE-ger)—very excited and interested

festival (FES-tuh-vuhl)—a celebration

maze (MEYZ)—a network of paths that connect with one another

trillium (TRIL-ee-uhm)—a plant that has three leaves and a single flower with three petals and that blooms in the spring

A-MAZE-ING

J.C. has a great time walking through
the maze of flowers at the Spring Flower
Festival. Imagine the maze he followed
from beginning to end. Then draw a picture
of it. Don't forget to include the great
white trillium he saw with Nana. You can
also draw the different flowers J.C. might
have seen along the way.

1. Have you ever gone to a special event, like the Spring Flower Festival, with your grandparents or other family members? Where was it, and what did you enjoy the most?

2. J.C. was excited about the Spring Flower Festival, but he also wanted to go to the zoo with Amir and Vicky. Have you ever had to choose between two things you wanted to do? How did you decide?

3. The story ends with J.C. giving Amir and Vicky friendship flowers. Imagine you are Amir or Vicky. What type of friendship gift would you find for J.C. at the zoo?

LET'S WRITE

1. J.C. lives close to his grandparents, which means they can do fun things together year-round. Write a list of activities J.C. could do with Nana and Pop-Pop. Include one activity for each season: winter, spring, summer, and fall.

2. J.C. and his family are delayed waiting for the train. Think about a time you were stuck somewhere. What superpowers would you use to make sure you got to your destination on time?

3. Different flowers grow in different parts of the world. Do some research to find the types of flowers that grow where you live. Then see if you can find one!

Dorothy H. Price loves writing stories for young readers, starting with her first picture book, *Nana's Favorite Things*. A 2019 winner of the We Need Diverse Books Mentorship Program, Dorothy is also an active member of the SCBWI Carolinas. She hopes all young readers know they can grow up to write stories too.

Shiane Salabie is a Jamaica-born illustrator based in the Philadelphia tristate area. When she moved to the United States, she discovered her first true love: the library. Shiane later realized that she wanted to bring stories to life and uses her art to do so.